THE PENGUIN POETS

ALL OF US HERE

Irving Feldman was born in Coney Island, New York. His poems have appeared in *The New Yorker, Harper's, The Atlantic Monthly, Grand Street, Partisan Review,* and other magazines, and his collections of poems to date include *Works and Days, The Pripet Marshes* (nominated for the National Book Award), *Magic Papers, Lost Originals,* and *Leaping Clear* (also nominated for the National Book Award). Mr. Feldman has earned numerous awards and grants, including a Guggenheim Fellowship and the National Institute of Arts and Letters Award. He is a professor of English at the State University of New York at Buffalo.

All of Us Here

Irving Feldman

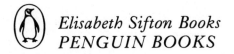

Elisabeth Sifton Books
PENGUIN BOOKS

ELISABETH SIFTON BOOKS · PENGUIN BOOKS
Viking Penguin Inc., 40 West 23rd Street,
New York, New York 10010, U.S.A.
Penguin Books Ltd, Harmondsworth,
Middlesex, England
Penguin Books Australia Ltd, Ringwood,
Victoria, Australia
Penguin Books Canada Limited, 2801 John Street,
Markham, Ontario, Canada L3R 1B4
Penguin Books (N.Z.) Ltd, 182–190 Wairau Road,
Auckland 10, New Zealand

First published in 1986 by Viking Penguin Inc.
in simultaneous hardcover and paperback editions
Published simultaneously in Canada

Some of the poems in this book first appeared in
*The New Republic, Shenandoah, Grand Street, Yale Review,
Confrontation, Southwest Review,* and *Iowa Review.*

LIBRARY OF CONGRESS CATALOGING IN PUBLICATION DATA
Feldman, Irving, 1928–
    All of us here and other poems.
    "Elisabeth Sifton books."
    I. Title.
PS3511.E23A79   1986b   811'.54   85-32017
ISBN 0 14 058.563 X

Printed in the United States of America by
R. R. Donnelley & Sons Company, Harrisonburg, Virginia
Set in Janson

To Katharine

CONTENTS

II

III   THE FLIGHT FROM THE CITY

IV

I ALL OF US HERE

All of Us Here

—OH, IT'S ALL SO

—Oh, it's all so obvious!

—They say this show got some terrific reviews.

—I swear I did a double-take when I came in.
Old SUBWAY SEATS, used TABLES, metal SCRAP!

—These statues are plaster casts of real people?

—To me it's like a wax museum.
—Of victims? That's a new one.

—I think I'll just take a peek at the gallery register.

—Do you have any idea what plaster does to a rug?

—What's this guy got that I don't have?
I'll tell you what. Connections, man, connections.

—God, sometimes I feel just the way they look.

—I think he sympathizes with people.
He must be a nice man.

—I don't know what it is about these statues . . .

—Where are the café jokes of yesteryear?
—They're in the classroom, wagging gray beards!

—It's starting to get crowded in here.
—Who are all these people?

OR THIS MIGHT BE OAFLAND

Or this might be Oafland, and these the local oaves
—Mr. and Mrs. and all the other Whites,
who are posing now in plaster clothes in a state
of cloddish wonderment, poor earth's brightest face
turned toward heaven by a random harrow tooth.
Oh but these must be city folk stranded among
a derelict flotsam of ruptured contexts,
sticks and stones from gray, forgettable neighborhoods
that we ourselves escaped ages and ages ago:
KITCHEN SINK, BUS SEAT, PARK BENCH, DINER TABLE,
RESTAURANT WINDOW, CAR DOOR, LADDER, PHONE BOOTH,
   BAR . . .
And so we're quick to sense our advantage here
where *they* seem both out of place and stuck forever
in their bored borough of the 'thirties and 'forties,
while *we* are elegant and up-to-the-minute,
can come and go, preen our intelligence,
eye them boldly from all sides and up close,
and pass remarks about them in loud voices
—*because they can't forbid us anything.*
Nor are we either all alike or all one piece,
white clothing on a whited skin.
                              And yet, and yet
for all this contrasting vividness we feel
—never so alive, alert, ardent, bright as now,
this wonderful fuss of being human and young!—
their lumpish solitude admonishes our limber
volubility, from moment to moment makes
halt crimped stuttering abashed old moody poor
the smooth lavishings and lappings of our beings,
which, like water, would caress equally everywhere.

In time, they will all be carted off and dispersed
to hotel atriums and to motel lobbies,
to new museums, statehouse courtyards, bus depots
—today, however, we are compelled to grant
their massed redundancy the power of earth:
we acknowledge that Being (however poor) precedes
becoming (though swift, exuberant, fascinating, gorgeous).

Here at dawn light and by nighttime's neon, before
our rising greetings began to swell and after
our goodbyes' *diminuendo* on the stairwell down,
they—though lacking our stylishness, charm, fervor,
gallantry, spirit, fine clothing, wit—are silent,
they are motionless, they are mineral, and white.
And therefore, in reluctant recognition of
an order of immobility so old
that death itself must seem the junior partner,
our rich laughter turns to chalk and powder
in our mouths, and we yield this place to them.

OH, HERE AND THERE

Oh, here and there one seems poised between paces,
ready perhaps to push on, though not to step out.
But mostly they stand, sit about, or lie down
—in the averaged postures of average people
reproduced in a kind of stiffened pudding
we sense is harsh, cold, unpleasant to touch.
Surely our time is not stillborn and devoid
of vividness—*some* bright spirits walk the earth,
please the eye, impress and charge the memory.
But these, always a shy step out of focus,
how apologetic these lagging figures seem,
and how little they claim, as if the life-size
into which they've been cast is sizes too large,
the soft and friable plaster too enduring,
their bleak monochrome still one color too many.
It's true they loom like revenants in their scenes,
old blanks, cut-outs, massive absences who want
to climb back into the world which keeps on going,
misfits trying to get at least *something* right,
who mime with dogged, solemn single-mindedness
this one's lopsided frown, that one's wrinkled suit.
Is this why suddenly we feel it disloyal
of us if we smile, stretch, straighten our clothes?
—But it is only now we notice it.
They have no eyes or their eyes are closed.

If we were gifted at flight, lyrical, blessed
with clairvoyance, able to see our way past all
this obviousness to the possible impossible,
we'd mind less their collapsed spectrum of the human,
this mirror of literalness (which reflects,

which cannot see) that they hold up to our eyes
—reminding us too tiresomely of our obtrusive,
too tedious, too obvious, too mortal selves.

To be responded to is as close as one
can come in *this* life to immortality.
So we come and stand here and look at them
to make more answering life to answer us
—though it's like calling on the outcast next door,
like watching the hermit in the store window . . .
or whatever glimmer of kinship brings us back to
the eyes of animals at the zoo . . . If only
these figures seemed aware of one another . . .
If we could paint our faces on the vacant stares . . .
Some strangers scattered together among some stones,
what welcomes us here is only ourselves in
a sudden vision of ourselves, as if a first life
we were torn from should rise and recollect itself
and be embodied in us . . . when our eyes meet:
a crowd of powers in a single being,
the one, composite body of everybody
—original through all its generations,
part of, symbol of, everything ever alive—
whose burgeoning members wave affably and nod,
answering each one's silent question, *Yes, yes,* and *yes!*
—"We all shall die, but will none of us be reborn?"

But no, but no, they are creatures of paste,
too-large dolls left back in the solitude
of some local but permanent interim
—the terminal moraine where time ran out—
who hope no longer to be born at all.
Here they stay thumping their numb dumb humdrums
—where nothing is wrong except everything,
and what isn't grimed is broken, and what
is unbroken is unendurable,
and resurrection dips a dirty spade,
adding dust to dust, piling ashes up.

OF COURSE, WE WOULD WISH

Of course, we would wish them angelic lookouts
on vigil to transmit—brightening and moving—
the glory still forthcoming, still pending . . .
alert geniuses of anticipation . . .
in the pure moment prior to speech. . . .

Sadly, it's the dead themselves they resemble,
no longer fussing to be served better and more,
withdrawing their demands on our attention,
and are humble suddenly and patient, keep
to their places, and make themselves smaller
to give death greater room, and hunch down farther.
It hurts to see them so decent and poor.
And it does no good to scold them for it,
to shout at these newly impoverished relations
crowding timidly in the narrow hallway,
or recall to them the old extravagance,
or tempt them back with favorite morsels
and the glowing tales that made the hearth warmer.
Not once more will they rise from the table
or come laughing out of the vestibule,
kicking the springtime's mud from their shoes.
The little and the less consume them now.
What a fever it is, to make do with nothing.
And throw off every word they ever wore,
the metaphors that made them legendary
—as if anything not literal bone, not plain
matter, was illusion, delirium, conceit,
swollenness of spirit prancing on show,
this corruption ailing in their ligaments now.

They are dying to be the letter itself:
immaculate, and perfect in form, minute,
not ever again to be read into,
and beyond whiteness white, sole, invisible.

THEY WERE NOT ALIVE

They were not alive and were walking in the streets,
or they were in a bus, sitting still, and still
were white all over, were stone in the core . . .
This white plague expresses now the new boundary
of death, senseless, superimposed, suddenly there,
down, up, right here . . . unstable, treacherous, *jumping.*
And the plainly given, the unconjectured
dimension—faithful, basic, calm and ancient—
the horizontal no longer symbolizes
the dead in their lying down in the earth,
and the air without dimension opening
and opening and opening over them.
No one goes to tend the bulbs and roots and rain,
and be our farmers in the under-soil
—our other people in our other country,
where, living and dead together, we raised up time
time and time again in the fruitful order of seasons.
And no place is left for us to go.
                         Shall we, too,
ride around and around in buses all day,
and clog the streets in our aimless white parade,
over and over, each telling himself over
the bargains, the bargains he found and didn't buy?
They keep on crowding in, hang on, get in the way
—like the pensioned-off milestones of America
come in from the distances to be *mementi mori.*
We'll never let that happen to us!
                         No way,
we say, thanks, but no thanks.

                        And that's why all of us

who can afford it walk in a corporation
of interferers, a cloud of professionals
we hire to give Calamity the runaround:
phantom limbs we throw the circling shark,
live prostheses we dangle at the octopus,
foreplay forever for the heartless fucker
—*mucho* funny stuff to tie Fate up in court
or in hospital, let it hemorrhage in the head
and break a spine before it gets at us and ours
—let it never leave Intensive Care on two feet!
Our experts' hubbub and consultants' *cha-cha-cha*
are going to make it damned expensive
to jump us in the dark and without a warning.
Why, just to know we're giving Trouble trouble helps.
And what a comforting sight your doctor is,
healthy and pink in a nice starched coat,
or your lawyer with your life in that envelope
he's having fun balancing on a fingertip,
while one crossed leg swings idly up, swings down,
and someone's insurance agent waves a fat check.
Their luck could rub off here, you never know,
and their immortality-of-office, why not?
—Our doctor's gonna die, but not with us,
our lawyer drop, but never in our place,
our priest lie down in—thanks—his own grave.
Yeah, if that's where the action is, we'll grab a piece,
take some tumbles up ahead of the big parade
with the rest of the white face, white collar clowns.
Am I my lawyer's doctor's priest's accountant's lawyer?
You can bet your bookie's life we hotshots
are flashing in and out of each other's shadow,
luring death toward us for the other guy and for
his palpitating fee—while our thumb jerks back
and our whisper tips, "*Him,* he's the one you're after.
I only *work* here. *He* put me up to it—he *hired* me!"

Because, let's face it, folks,
we'll never be together again after this.

OR PERHAPS IT'S REALLY *THEATER*

Or perhaps it's really *theater* of deprivation,
and here we've wandered onto a movie set
mocked up from famous stills of fifty years ago,
and we're free to walk around and rub elbows with
these lucky white stand-ins for the tardy stars.
Why, of course, we could be extras here ourselves!
And look, there's the strange moment before the MIRROR,
the gruesome all-nighter around the KITCHEN TABLE,
the DOORWAY where she threw him that funny look
that stayed with him his first weeks off in the army.
At last we'll get to see the backsides of everything,
and find out maybe what really was going on
—no poverty so poor it has no secrets!
And so, having these scenes for our inspection, at
our disposition, is sexy, exciting,
here's fame and nostalgia and something else precious:
seeing the machinery and yet not losing
the illusion . . .

But haven't we seen this flick before?
You know, the one where . . . right out of the 'thirties
. . . the bodies sagging among CHAIRS and WASHSTANDS
or plodding by COFFEE URNS and BUTCHER BLOCKS
through the grainy atmosphere, and gloom that suggests
perpetual confinement to amateurishness
. . . these coercive images of life after hope
. . . a century's terror by sentimentalism
freights the scene with yet blacker glooms of bad faith
—since candor alone is lighthearted—
somewhere a butcher's blunt finger is rending hearts,
while, faint, sweet, *crescendo* from the phantom soundtrack,

the still, sad music of humanism—so-called—
is symphonizing on the dark Stalinist fiddles . . .
Yes, the little people are appealing to *us*
to lead them into history . . . are dying to enlist
in the great cause of our generosity,
and, cap in hand, they come to us and say
with a shy dignity we simply can't resist,
"Here, good sirs, is all of our misery
—do with it, please, as you see fit."
. . . Careers open to idealism!

It all comes back, however faint, that redolence
of another era, but with the smugness cuddly,
the deception almost affectionate, affordable,
almost a joke—somber and improbable camp
that feels right at home in our living room.

Whatever can we be so famished for?

THE BYSTANDER AT THE MASSACRE

1

The bystander at the massacre of innocents
might have seen his own innocence among the dying
had not his distance from the spectacle of slaughter
(not all that far off, really) given him the space
to entertain a doubt—while it wrenched time backward
and made everything appear unalterable and past
even as everything kept on racing ahead.
He might not believe or come in time to what he saw.

Murderers and babies and frenzied howling mothers,
everyone crowded forward onto the picture plane
when he dropped to a knee to steady the camera
—yes, they could come this far but not a breath farther,—
and now, for all their mutual horror and panic,
their cudgels and knives and the scream-saturated sky,
they are unable to smash their way out, although
repeatedly he stabs his finger into the photo
as if to verify something incredible there
or at least to render the illusion palpable.

For his is the spectator's essential doubtfulness,
this feeling that among the sum of appearances
something important doesn't appear, and may never.
At precisely his distance—standing by, looking on—
he can't get close enough ever to be certain
reality isn't some extraordinary matter
not yet glistening on those dull upturned faces,
that running about, or gray sky ceaselessly screaming.
Of course he *knows*—who *doesn't* know?—even *we* know
that terrible things are going on out there.

2

Is it curiosity? or a kind of revery?
or recollection of the city-dweller's pastime,
watching people busily, simply, living in their lives
—what can have stopped us here, like angel emissaries
to a doomed town, to view them while they muse or walk
about or work at their machines on a sunny day
torn from the archives of the ordinary?
Their entire absorption in whatever they're doing,
the feats of diligence and attending by which
they materialize, and gather in, being
—it seems recreation enough to observe them,
and almost a blessing that they take us for granted,
our gaze unchallenged, undeflected by any other,
as if, unseen, absorbed in our purest looking now,
we, too, could enter their sustained communion
and this moment should become the life we are living.
And so it's oddly flattering to feel welcomed
by being ignored, as if we belong here like stones
and trees, are features natural to the scene,
and haven't come this way disengaged, freewheeling
between one city burning and another's tinder,
and with that uproar—our names screaming—always
in our ears.

      Each in glowing concentration here:
the one of the DOORWAY, the one of the TABLE,
the one of the RESTAURANT WINDOW, the other one
and the other one and the other one, and each one
stitching, tapping, a little by a little
making it indubitable and good,
an artisan of the whole creation
as it was—streaming ether of their concern
for one another—before the slaughterers came.
Before the slaughterers come,
we can have no other way
but to make our way back

into the city, into the center
where what happened is happening now

—or our evasion expands to enormous
complicity, explodes in the spectator's rage
and demented scream for more bigger quicker death,
and we rush toward the time when, not lifting a finger
—and yet we may fairly claim it our creation,—
we spectators are gathered into the act
and—for a second's intimate stupendous fraction—
everything is beyond any doubt real.

THE WHIRLWIND WE WOULDN'T ENTER

The whirlwind we wouldn't enter of our names
beseeching us from the sky . . . is far away now,
thunder over Disney Village to which we've come
. . . a green room somewhere in the wings of its heaven
where enchanted souls in whitewash await their cues
—the proto-Mickey, as it were, and ur-Donald—see,
there's Hughie Human, Percy Person, Cindy Citizen
in Santa's workshop before the color goes on for good
. . . to illuminate within the nihilist blindness
the sentimental vision . . . and look, we're kids again!
simple and pure in heart, healed, grateful that we're us
—because right now nothing ever really happened,
and life never asked more of us than innocence—
our new eyes behold not absence but color, our ears
hear Mickey's sweet squeak, Donald's stormy funny grumble!

Mickey and Donald want us to be happy,
they'll do anything to make us smile, laugh, clap our hands
—look how silly and harmless, not big and scary,
they make themselves for our sakes, we *have* to laugh
—because they love us as we are . . . happy, being good,
and want us never to be any other way.
Wide is our way and lined with clowns from here to forever,
from kindergarten to life and back again.
All we have to do is to enjoy the entertainment
and watch our mouths on the monitor screeching out loud.
It's hilarious and fun and interesting, too.
Donald is famous, but Mickey is famouser.
They can make *anyone* be charming to them.
Just because of who they are. It's magic.
How no one's boring, mopey, dopey, ugly, rude.

They'll even come to where we are and walk around
like living statues bigger than life and shake our hands.
"Hi, Mickey!" "Hi, Donald!" we practice on their names
over and over, even when they're not around.
And Mickey loves Donald and Donald Mickey just the same
because they're in the family of everyone famous,
who everyday spend their time being nice to each other.
They go back and forth into their houses to visit,
and still whenever they meet in restaurants and places,
it's just like they haven't seen each other in years.
And all the time they're getting and giving out prizes.
You can see from their smiles they're completely sincere.
We love you, Mickey and Donald, with all our hearts.
And we'll never change. We promise.
For all you give us, it's the least we can do.

Sweet puppy self-love, the paradise of white lies is
the one paradise always in our power to achieve.

SURELY THEY'RE JUST SO LARGE

Surely they're just so large as their burdens allow,
and no smaller—yet—than the task at hand requires.
But when the light is right these figures of old earth
—the stooped pedestrian, the huddled subway rider—
are roused in their sad ghetto of anachronism
by today's untoward sun—and we see we've rolled down
the abyssal slope to a lost academy,
some dusty museum basement where plasters of
the classics have slept tumbled about cheek by jowl
in nameless peace all the minutes of these centuries:
heroes, athletes, titans in everyday clothing
who come racing in place from all the way back
to stand in no time at all—all of them, all of us
together here—at the abandoned finish line,
our fleet forerunners in prospective elegy,
champions, pioneers of the missing future:
this Laocoön braced against the supple void,
Atlas bearing up under a genocide or so,
and Sisyphus, his sleeves rolled, ready now to start
getting that apocalypse out of the cellar

—the stooped pedestrian, the huddled subway rider,
such shadows flung at speed of light across the world
by enormity, just peeping around the corner.

NATIVE SOIL, WE SAY

Native soil, we say. But soil is debris,
blasted or broken loose, carried off, deposited,
its affiliations casual, crumbling
—a huddle of strangers from the old country,
arriving by wind or ferried over on
the water, carried away again . . . Of such
alluvium we are formed.

          Our voluble streets
send the natural drift careening forward
at unnatural speed. You can glimpse the smashup
down any awful *cul de sac* you're driven past
—a litter of outmoded styles, old headlines,
fungible events, public gossip, rubbish news,
the *caca*-literature we generate, consume.
This is the slang and hot slurry of time, at once
traffic jam (trapped by one another, jeering)
and freeway shooting range of zooming moments
—the medium where you dare not set your foot once.
The rotting of the homeland's establishments
lays bare—underneath—our condition as clay;
nomads of words, our urban vanity is
our freedom of speech, the booming rumor of names
on which we make our getaway from earth
toward the high, airless, astral zones of fame.
A multitudinous gabble sweeps us along
—our ambition is to let nothing go unsaid—
while we go on talking as much as we can,
keeping up with what we accelerate.

*   *   *

Some obscure nostalgia for dumbness and earth,
for easeful insignificance, draws us back
to these dioramas of a vanished species
pasturing in half-dismantled habitats
—archaeological digs, you might say,
of the old neighborhood a generation back,
providing views of the crude artifacts,
the charming and un-selfconscious folkways,
a vision of life without the fuss of life.
How odd they didn't foresee their anachronism.
Now they seem revived a bit by the fracturing
that frames—and refreshes—each *mise-en-scène*.
And if these figures don't exactly welcome us
—but it wasn't precisely them we left behind,—
they seem, well, to have left a place for us.
How easily we take our stations beside them,
near the SUBWAY SEAT, at the COFFEE SHOP COUNTER.
It feels funny but right—we fit here,
we fit right in. Whatever our bewilderment,
our fear of having checked too much at the door,
our bodies, at least, have forgotten nothing,
except how deeply they mourned these other bodies.
So this is how it always was,
how it has always been meant to be,
the kingdom that should have been our heritage,
this pastoral standstill we've returned to flesh out,
reviving the *cultures mortes* as *tableaux vivants*.

Our soil is technological—our things, our ways
with things, our words about them—but rich and deep.
These are bits of pulverized place we pose among,
the solemn junk that was New Jersey and the Bronx,
and shall be what land our shatterings are lofted toward.

DUST, PALLOR, DRABNESS

Dust, pallor, drabness of the tomb.
                            The air in here
feels dated, stale, as if some special apparatus
—spiritual gills, say—were needed to get
into our lungs what little uncombusted time
is left, someone's been embezzling it so long.
These plasters, perhaps?
                            Impossible! Dis-animate,
they look like coprolites, a species of giant dung
left whitening on the ground with dignity and age
—of what unimaginable, departed gods
the sacred excrement, divine residuum?
No one else is around—just them and us.
Or not quite—there are the *things* they live among:
LADDER, SHOWER STALL, DENTAL CHAIR, BUS DOOR, EASEL . . .
Entirely literal beings of wood, glass, metal,
they lord it over the poor torpid people,
hardly persons at all, crude plaster copies
and nameless except for their jobs, locales, or gestures.
Surely, we feel, they were entombed to accompany
and attend these Things, their brilliant masters, in
the after-world—as we, perhaps, do in this one.
A little lower than the Things, are these figures,
are we ourselves, just minor matter, *choses manquées?*
—lacking their hardness and impassivity,
their quietly unanxious single-mindedness,
their on the whole cheerful sense that things turn out,
sometimes someone boards a BUS, someone else climbs a LADDER.

It seemed rude of us and wrong—a profanation—
to come barging in on their cryptic privacy

with our contemporary bulk and breathlessness
to cast this public light over their dusty lives
and lesser idols from the Age of Industry.
But now a second thought suggests we are indeed
the after-world they always intended to reach.
It's touching, really, heartening and heartbreaking
at once, that all this was arranged for our eyes.
Then we're not some grayed-out weed-choked local stop
the splendid silver *Rapido* of their Time Capsule
would always be roaring and barreling past
on its shining errand with important cargo,
but the very Terminus for which it set forth
aeons and aeons—a whole decade!—ago.
And how well we understand this—we, too, wish
only to be immortal in their modest way:
to be delivered in time to be tomorrow's news.
—See yourselves in us and weep, free us and be glad!

Wherever we are, whatever place this is, it, too,
is in transit, thing after thing flashing by, falling
into the past—for us immortality can't be
to last forever but to have a second chance,
another time over the littered quickening ground,
one more try at getting into the flow . . .

Skeptic time runs through and discards this and that,
goes through everything in time, as, in this case,
the glamor of sheer materiality.
These Things are less impressive than they should be,
or *were* when, reigning lords, they were launched toward us.
And if they thought to fall to earth like saviors
with final words on single Form and simple Being,
it seems to us now no great thing to be a Thing,
of rather less importance than the flux
and prompt delivery of information about it.
Painful, but the enchantment was lost in transit
—only some beat-up old secondhand furniture
has come bumping down.

And after all, we *have* gone on:
children of change, our birthright is skepticism
—total and unearned, but paid for afterward.
Like a man who ten minutes too late clutches at
his lifeless pocket—Oh my god, the wallet's gone!—
we gasp wildly as if to ask the fugitive air,
for lack of anything else to accuse,
What have you left us that we could wish to endure?

ALONE, ALIVE IN A TOMB

Alone, alive in a tomb, who doesn't dream
of despoliation?
        —The sudden shockpower of
impunity: these leavings are helpless, they're *loot*
—let's grab it, let's go! And then the hot sweet
transfusing firewater of something-for-nothing
is like an extra life, like *more* life in the veins.
We're bigger, fiercer, twice as many as when
we came running in just ahead of wind and fire.
That was something—we really got our asses singed!
And look at us now: fine, fat, free, *untouchable.*
Whatever grocer god left this sweet stash, it's ours.
We'll put the useless stiffs to work: our land
factory livestock slaves—we'll milk them good.
Inside their suits our nakedness will be in business.
And it's all good stuff, man—it's *merchandise.*
Hey, they should be happy we save their heritage.
So let's go for it, let's cash in again quick!
And just for luck we'll dump a pile and leave it,
a love-note to this here immaculate horror,
a message from the good guys: *Goombye—and thanks!*
And we *gone.* See, wind die way down, fire black out.
It quiet, real quiet, outside . . . Shh . . . you hear that?
—*Who, regarding the dead, does not feel himself*
as purely needy, as simply honest as a flame?

But suppose that dream of our survival's a joke
and we've really been kidding ourselves along,
that we didn't just step in here to escape
a sudden shower or the street's whirling-burly,
but by some fluke—I know this sounds crazy—

it's *we* who are transfixed in a trance so deep
that everything around has stopped dead in its tracks.
Only Terror moves . . . its million eyes over us,
slithering toward the final advent of fire
—that twice before made a city its cenotaph
and scared us into this impersonation of stone.
If we should move, the world would end,
but the end of the world is us not moving.
The burning jelly everywhere is united
in a single burning, a single eye.
Inspector Fire looks us over.
The moment of the end is unending ash.
Illumination we dare not move to utter.

Nothing stands outside the dream—unless that is you.
Look at us, don't you see what we're trying to say?

LOVELY TIMES, HEROIC

Lovely times, heroic decades, happiness.
These we offer up to claws and kindling,
to the fierce gods who covet flame,
the prosperous with their sweet tooth.
Sacrifice is our panacea,
even for the illness of being well.
And this science comes so naturally,
measuring out ourselves for immolation.
The ash we keep: the bad nights, failure,
wasted years numbered in the catalogues
of discontent we poormouth at heaven.
And our deliberate evil, isn't this
our last *hopeful* offering to a god
who has despised our goods?
                              Take them! Take these!
Take me! we cry to any possible spirit,
finding ourselves uncertain, fearful,
a stranger in trespass on a god's ground.
Millennia later we are latecomers still,
squatters fit to be driven off by
trembling earth and thunder of the just disaster.
Something in us howls with the gods against us
even as they blow our bewildered cities down.

Hearing ourselves as we think the gods must
—our mimicries of divine displeasure,
our *amor fati* raging to become
fuel in the gut of the greatest power,
our cry to make us light without remainder,—
no wonder we beg the elements, *Restore*

the chaos of your overwhelming concord!
No wonder we're merciless to each other.

Led off a little way from life,
and splashed with white all over,
symbolizing exsanguination,
prepared and yet to be offered,
or offered and not yet taken:
all of them halted halfway between
the world and the consummation.
And we feel we should do something about them,
bring them back to life, perhaps
—or step forward with them into the fire,
sensing ourselves also to be
sacrifices in search of a god.

—IT'S OBVIOUS OBVIOUS

—It's obvious obvious obvious!

—That one is so strange and sad,
I'd like to adopt it, give it a nice home.
—There you go again.

—Go ahead, call her up.
What have you got to lose?

—Is George Segal a famous sculptor?
—You bet he's famous.

—Mommy, I don't see any children statues.

—A beautiful day like today.
We could be in Bloomingdale's right this minute.

—Well, you took your time showing up.
—I'm skipping lunch just to be here now.

—We'll have to come back when it's not so crowded.
—This is the first time I haven't seen someone I know.

—I've had enough of you and your yapping.

—Did you hear what I heard?

—I like the way the line of this arm goes
with that leg, and with the beige TABLE. *See?*
—That's really fascinating.
Are you an artist yourself?

*   *   *

—My doctor said to stick with the treatments.
—Come on, you're kidding!

—Look, the sun's out.
Can I buy you a drink?

—Are you sure you're warm enough in that raincoat?

THE LIGHT THAT TOOK THE SNAPSHOT

The light that took the snapshot of the world
shows them—with a clarity not granted in
this life—poised in sober expectation at
the intersection of the ordinary and
of Something Very Important, which has stopped them
to ask the way, then turns back with a question,
What were you doing when the world ended?

The woman in the RESTAURANT WINDOW is saying,
I was lost in thought, and then
I was just about to lift the cup
when I saw the wavelets in the coffee
that were the world ending

And the driver of the TRUCK,
I noticed the signal was changing
and then saw up ahead the end of the world

The PRINTING PRESS operator says,
I was busy freeing up a lever
that ended the world

SIMPLE OUTLINES, HUMAN SHAPES

Simple outlines, human shapes, daily acts, plain poses
—exhibits for the Museum of Humanity,
the place to take the kids on Sunday outings and show them
how it must have been to be, once upon a time,
a common man in the Century of the Common Man.
"Eternal" and homely, final but merely roughed out,
gentle and not to be budged from their perplexity,
and blanching still in the calamitous afterglow,
they're like completed destinies that are at the same time
just poor people who couldn't get out of the way,
whose names have been exalted into allegory:
Exile, Homeless, Refugee, Unknown, Mourner, Corpse.

And if we surround and see them from every side,
all the while we can't help putting ourselves in their places,
suffer for them their vulnerability to our eyes.
Life, defenseless life—with nothing left to defend!
We understand: so everything must be looking at us
with the sight that seeing too much burned from our gaze.
And if we, too, now lack inner refuge and outer force,
are the very horror your generation strolls among,
we *will* arise from these tombs of hoarfrost and ash
—if only for the children's sakes who've led us here
by the hand, and over and over touch their small faces
and crusted staring eyes to our stone fingertips—
we swear it . . .

—Surely they are saying over and over again
inside their black white silence *something* like this.
But what they suffered, they also did,
and we can't find it in our hearts to pity, or forgive.

STRETCHED OUT AT LENGTH

Stretched out at length on the ground
—one might think them dreamers in a meadow,—
how young they all appear now,
as yet unbent into characters,
but as if at any moment they
may climb, grown and whole, out
of the cracked open molds, and step
lightly into other worlds . . .
Who wouldn't follow them there!
But their dust is old,
earth is old and craves
a sense for its shambles,
why it should be this and only
this broken, low horizon of clods
the empty furrow cast up
in the course of defining itself.

And we, have we no sense to offer
to ease the torment of this earth?
—standing here, craning necks, squinting,
twisting ourselves half upside down over
the puzzle of these foreshortenings,
these fevered limbs, knobs, bulges like
the scrabbled ware of a potter's field.
But for all our triumphs of contortion,
we can't resolve the clutter into
figures intelligible like ourselves.
Or they refuse to make themselves clear.
A hidden life—turned low to endure—
persists in there, and contends with us,
with itself, with *everything*

for the meaning of the life.
And will not let us rest
though we pursue it down through
the last scattering
                    —ourselves suddenly
landlocked here, at our limit,
grappling for our own coherence
among clots of dirt, rock, soil . . .

Even as we rouse ourselves
from the spell of earth,
even as we straighten up and start
to disperse and move on to other things
—something, perhaps to gather
itself in prayer, perhaps
to touch its life
to the life of dust,
something sinks to its knees in us,
something falls all the way
and doesn't stop.

THIS COUPLE STROLLING HERE

This couple strolling here beside the BRICK WALL
look the way we might look if it were us
in raincoats walking slowly in the city dusk
—but how much better at it these figures are!
Their effortless mastery of the clichés
of everyday life—which we, who almost never
fit in anywhere, seem to go on missing—
serves them perfectly again and again,
when they sit down side by side on a PARK BENCH
or lie in BED and twine peacefully together.
They always manage to achieve the right pose,
without insistence or abashment or cleverness,
a gesture left over or one aspired toward.

We should envy them, no? Immortality
experienced from within must seem just such
imperturbable ordinariness as theirs,
repose deep in the simple heart of averageness,
which death, raiding along the frontier, must take
forever to reach.
                    The eternal verity of
their middle way nourishes with safety and seemliness.

Then *ils sont dans le vrai?* Well, it feels that way,
as if a truth too large for us to see at once
has brought our bodies to fall in alongside theirs
in easy, even, companionable pacing.
We go along. Turn and look again. And all go on
together. So, we think, it *is* possible
to be comfortable, large, happy, in the right.
And it grows on one!

The mirror they hold up to us
is tempered with a gentle curve of revery.
And whether it's they or ourselves we see
doesn't much matter. Whoever's there—presence
and person and apparition and absence,
the once, the actual, the not yet, the never—
we don't want to be halted by identities,
we want to go on becoming in wonder.
About these figures we don't ask, "Who are they?"
We ask, "Who, who is it they remind us of?"

DID THEY LOVE ONE ANOTHER?

Did they love one another? Were they good?
So we ask about them, the old ones, the old people,
these questions that abandoned children send
toward the dark to follow their elusive families.
—Even the child whose way the stars made plain
may never be certain his coming was awaited
or that he is himself the child they intended.
But we're no longer children, have children of
our own and some title to this ground, these walls
—and yet find ourselves on a dark road downward
on an urgent errand to an uncanny past
after the fugitive powers through which
we are at all and may be reborn, renewed.
But it is so difficult to understand
the coherence of, say, fifty years ago,
to see that theirs was a world entire and not
a scattering of stray evidences, odd things
worn with use, habituated to their presence,
enriched with their sociability . . . this chair,
or this cup chipped, mended, left behind, this table . . .
If we could go back and see them as they were . . .

Then recall them in the time of their strength,
the brothers and sisters then, their husbands and wives,
the landsmen, the large neighbors, the friends—as if
each one were a country and all of them the world!
Remember their enthusiasms, ceremonies, card
games, big voices, jobs, what headlines, politicians,
comics, rumors, music moved them, what laughter, and
how seriously they took each other and themselves
and us, and were wholly and profoundly at one with

the terrors and trivia of the century.
Heartstopping to see it this clearly now:
bone, soul and song, they belonged to their time,
refuse to be transported into any other.
And dwindle as we look, move away farther, lost
at last among the multitudes of the era,
unknown in the crumbling society of clay,
the sands of the earth where we scratch, inquire . . .
How small our giants were and by how many had
been multiplied to become historical!

And then remember how we looked for them among
the horde on park benches as if in some sunlit
encampment of sorrows beside a black ocean
—their white heads like every other white head,
their clothes, coat for coat, dress for dress, the same,
their voices as low and unevocative.
A dog that day—had they a dog—their little dog
would, without a second's delay and joy
in each leaping step, have found them right away,
though barking through the sky of a whole galaxy!
But we, blind in the sameness and the sameness,
could not imagine by what power they
—so small, so indistinguishable themselves—
had singled us out from among the vague unborn,
and seen in each one the one original
each of us knows is named in his name alone.

But even there in the land of the dead,
lost not in time but out of it, in timelessness,
among the quiet, whited and nonchalant crowds,
where nothing moved but our shadows' vague passage,
a steady gaze of recognition from afar,
the happy affection glowing in those eyes
as we approached, announced who lit our way
and who it was there among so many:
it was they, themselves, and we were ourselves!
To have found cause, in such a place, for celebration!

Then *See, see who's here!* their eyes said in greeting.
And *Only you were missing, the last to arrive.*
Look, now there's not an empty chair at the table!
their eyes exclaimed what their voices could not
—while we looked into the bright heart of living coal
from our cold threshold in the bitter white dark.
And, heaping our eyes with their gift, each time
and time and time again they send us forth.

THEY SAY TO US

They say to us in quiet voices,
matter of fact, hushed with feeling
(to which we murmur our responses),
Here, this is the one.
Of course, you never met him.
And this is his wife.
This one is her brother.
He *passed on a year ago July.*
Here she's holding her eldest.
You can see she's pregnant.
That would have been
with little William . . .
To which we murmur,
Yes, yes, I see.
I see him. I see her.
Yes, takes after the father . . .
No, I never met him.
So, that's *the brother!*
Where is she now?
We are passing photos from hand to hand,
the living and the dead,
who mingle here
as nowhere else.
Almost we heft
the squares of shining paper
on our palms as if
to ponder better
their weight of being.
And yes, truly, they
appreciate under our gaze,
augment in our considering.

It is all very important.
This ritual is profound,
solemn, religious—we feel it,
become weighty ourselves,
judicious, like gods:
even and merciful in judgment,
simple, courteous and worthy.
Now we hand the photos back.
There they are—"little William,"
"her brother," "the neighbor's girl"—
all of them pressed close
in a single pack in dark
and radiant density.
All of us here
are deeply satisfied.

II

Our Father

In memory

This stranger whose flesh we never ate,
who, rather, sat at table with us, eating,
who for our sakes clothed himself in pelts like ours
and went away far all times to everywhere until,
clambering down starways into our street,
he stood in the door, the dusk-loaf under his arm,
and unpacked the lamplight of the parlor corner
where he called us to him and told us we were his,
and lost in thought led away our little army
of mimics to parade the deep lanes of silence.
Of our mother we ate always and plentifully,
her body was ours to possess and we did so,
thoughtlessly, yes, and also in adoration.
But how shall we understand this stranger?
And how are we ever to make amends to him?
—who had the power to eat us and didn't,
who consented to abide in one house with us,
and hailed the sun down to make the dinner hour,
and bid bread to rise daily out of white dust,
peopling it with mysterious vacancies,
and new night after old washed the odd smells
from himself with sleep and forgot his strangeness
and was, one moment at dawn, little again,
hungry like us, like us waiting to be fed.
How then can we renew his acquaintance, that boy
lost in the man, this man missing in the world,
walking among all that must be inexplicable?
And how are we to thank him properly?
who salted our cheerful, selfish tongues with farewell,
and gave us his name to ponder, to pass on, to keep.

River

Swift at its outset, ebullient.
And later on a wide majesty.
And always irresistible to itself.
And here, flow on its flow, the moments chose
to mirror themselves—or were helpless not
to be refashioned on its wayward glass.
High, up-ended clouds unloosed
their tumble of images, swallows were
at dusk and dawn, and wherever
someone looked
the moon went wavering,
the dark old towns swam slowly at its edges.
Day after day, seeing's brave flotilla
rode entranced on its motioning.
Whole civilizations found their trope
in its character and progress.

Under that,
and under that all,
it is feeling a way,
sightless, dark, small,
mere water
moving by touch, trickling
in fine deviations, in
precise intimations.
It gravitates
toward, it values, each
suddenness and resisting.
Stone, snag, hollow,
one by one
—it comes and savors them

as it can, disturbs minutely
to be saying, *Stranger? Or
friend? Do you prefer
to stay? Or come along?
Here, let me see if I
can help you on.*
                    Mentioned,
mulled in its divinations,
the old things startle into
life after life, entering
the water's disseminations.
The rusting auto and charred pleasure
craft, this silted loop of tire
—what we have abandoned,
or is abandoning us,
is the knowledge by which
the water goes along.
And had it words,
the water would say it is joy
to know the grain by grain
of its ground and, knowing it,
to be beginning
afresh.

An Atlantiad

Who is this great poet lapping near our feet?
—this shaggiest dog that ever swam ashore
and shook its coat dry onto the dull pebbles.
The Atlantic itself? at Rockaway Beach?
Mumble master of toneless sublimities,
who won't stick to a point or even get to one,
always talk-talk-talking with its mouth full
—impossible to tell just what it feels
and, therefore, to understand why it goes
on and on about itself so, and in
some clunk's vocabulary restricted to
the slurps, thumps, bangings, rumbles and whooshes
of onomatopoeia.
Like a drunk trying to count his wad of dough,
this big lug is all thumbs and tongues,
helplessly unable to divide sound
from sense, or content from form, "organic"
with a vengeance, and woozily puttering
its fluent thumbprint over every shore.
Like the ungifted who invariably swear
(hand on heart before Art's customs agents),
"I only write for myself," it achieves
an exclusive sufficiency, which—whenever
we sit on the beach or wherever we dip
into it—goes on "relating to itself."
And why *does* it prefer its company to ours?
Surely it hasn't arranged this exhibition
—in broad, horizontal, full-color
centerfold nudity—just to be looked at!
Of course, one happily concedes its "greatness,"
and one did come prepared to admire—still

we might wish for less conceit, oh, a touch
of vanity, say, some little hankering
to hear applause, a wink of willingness
to, well, uh, meet us part way, and put aside
the indulgences of its "song of oneself."
—Obsessed old salt blubbering to our damp lapels
flecked with by-spray and bad breath from its brine maw.
Tell me, What damn duck did we ever do in
to be pummeled by all this humorlessness?
The bore is father to the solipsist:
feeling unperceived—since unresponded to—
one loses confidence in "reality."
Oh we might call it "awful big poet," except,
unwilling to say anything large by way
of any little, it lacks, precisely, scale,
being a multitude of behaviors
that can't or won't get an act together.
And how can we know this poet from its poem?
—with its naturalism of mental contents,
its "whatever I happen to be thinking now,"
its queasy slipslop of selves, wobbling riffraff
of fish and turds and tarballs, of orange rind
and old hats, kelp and tires and glittery grit
—all this churning visionary trivia
and stuff, this "stream-of-unconsciousness,"
this lost topography that's left us "all at sea,"
this pounding platitudes into subtleties,
this diluting any old sludgy cliché
to the palest world-hue, this everlasting
running running running running away . . .
Oh, too grand to blush for its banalities,
and grandly disdaining fastidiousness
—this poem that cannibalizes all its texts,
look at it guzzle the palimpsest of foam!—
incapable of pretense, of stepping back,
as we do, and taking thought, of putting
itself into (for example) *our* leaky shoes,
it ignores us perhaps from fear that we

may interrupt its droning and give it pause,
impose the artifice of closure, and beginning ...

But, say, who are those whatchamacallits way
out there, lumping the immaculate horizon?
Are they waterbabies? Or shipwrecks, God forbid?
Or seals? Or weltering scows? Or old pickled
imagery and symbols come up for air?
And what do they want? Are they coming here?
Oh no! ...
Oh yes! ...
Oh no! ... Oh *now*
we see them—sun
flashing on ... on flukes! and fabulous
cloudy tall—oh yes!—occasional *plumes*,
and black drums ... like ... oil-filled brows.
We hear elaborate soundings now,
sweet, sonorous terminologies.
Oh yes!
—it is a band of deepwater critics
and ocean-going scholars being buoyed
by boredom where you and I would simply drown.
And splash about, expounding water in
solemn, angelic vocabularies—in which
it's quite impossible *not* to be profound.
See, the sea receives these green redundancies
(slow, sleek, enormous emerald tons of cud)
—the swell of their tide is sweeping this way,
over the wavering, poor, historical sands.
But does it mean to engulf us, our humble
perspective, our merely personal view?
Down!
Down, I say!
Back off, cold beast!
Damn you, get off my feet!
Turn me loose, I said!
Though in to my knees, and up to my waist
—Oh my God, I can't swim!—

my armpits, my neck, and over my chin,
I fight on.
How dare you quote me!
And without permission!
I swear, if it's the last thing I do,
I'll sue. . . .

The Judgment of Diana

Blesse us then with wishèd sight.

1

After the slamming door downstairs had rattled shut
and excluded her along with the oblate moon
and darkness and leaves scurrying in the street,
long afterward, her archangel's pallor, pure,
disembodied, chill, lingered in the half-lit room
—the young never quite know when to leave—
rougeless lips as if bled dry, her eye
bright blue and unitalicized, that timbre
—unplaceably estranged,—her stilted voice,
the spooky, expressionless, would-be baritone.
In surplus army jacket and green fatigues
(did they camouflage a lurking roundness of thigh?),
those work shoes strictly for show; graceful almost,
spare, strapping, tall, she'd seemed a spear carrier
of Diana's out slumming on the night shift
to spread, *noblesse oblige,* her godawful pall
of radical solemnity—or was it,
after all, just the old gloom of forest and fen?
But suppose she *was* off somewhere laughing at us
now, back, say, on Artemis—or whatever
her pitiful planet was called—laughing . . .
if laughter ever transfigured that grim
utopia's ecstasy of being right . . .
her voice bassooning in a lost green glade,
or rocky enclave, its tale about how
those bad old dads had nearly got her
—while, self-exiled in their nunnery in the wild,
the martyr brides of ideology,
maddened by the crimes and misdeeds of men,
crouch nodding and snickering over some bones.

"The bastards! The shits!" they would be hissing—and
they would be right.
                              But my companions that night ...
did they, too, eavesdrop on that imagined scene?
And saw themselves with her implacable gaze
still eyeing us from the vacant chair?
And saw our ordinariness bemonstered by
the savage banalities of caricature?
—loose, clubby, bickering, comfortable, sort of,
with our insider's tolerance and gossip,
our vested disappointments and tenured failings,
middle-aged cogs lazily getting around
by rubbing elbows and scratching backs,
Charles, Andrew, Arthur, Melvin, Sidney, myself,
our gang of professor-poets who'd gathered,
as we did each year in leaf-troubling November,
to police a corner of the culture-feedlot,
swapping old nags or pushing a pet ape
—poets we hired to come say their verses—
by way of exchanging, with all due gravity,
our cards, scumbly and dog-eared, of identity
—Charles, Arthur, Andrew, Melvin, Sidney, and I.
Wherever pigeonholes are, pigeons must be,
and spats and bespatterings of the dovecote
—a roocooing featherweight hierarchy—
where, hoisted on the shoulders of the years
to our modest perches, we loafed alright
in a living room, each of us floating out
upon the perilous divan of his dossier,
or *vita*'s leaky pneumatic pouf, out along
the whirling margin of a great unknown.

2

                              God knows
what that lone student rep was doing there
—saving the world? or us from ourselves?
(and if so, to what end?) or doing right
for womankind? or for poetry?

Certainly,

salvation obsessed the air around her
—as if everywhere the *bête blanche* she hunted
must be vanishing into any stirring leaf
—as if these millennarian centuries
had made each breath she held climactic:
The End of History would simply not abide
one more course of after-dinner sherries!
—or exempt an evening of cozy politics.
I suppose—no, *of course!*—her zeal discommoded,
and we resented the judgment it implied
—she meant to save *us?* to save the world *from* us?—
and were bemused how she confided in her powers,
envied the years she'd have to learn better,
envied her the passionate singleness
that draws the bow and sets the arrow straight
—however its conceit may stultify the aim.
Page-like, princely, in her androgyny,
image of our youth surviving to mock us,
surely she accused this too palpable gender,
in which we were decaying, *of* which we
were dying—rams, bucks, bulls, boars flabbed out
from domestication, all those hot dashes
to the fat trough and shoving a way in first,
getting and begetting. And she asked for nothing
—was our patronage not worth the charming?—
refused to play weak daughter or warm darling,
to have us old bullies set between her and harm
our moral authority, our mortal bodies.
Then she would be intruder and stranger both?
—with the menace of one, the other's nakedness?
Who or what was she really? Why had she come?
And now her liability inflamed us?
Whom bully doesn't guard, bully will batter?
So one saw her—mere girl, the creature itself
divested of allure or standing—and glimpsed
in her *our* nakedness and estrangement, *our*

jeopardy, works swept into nothing, words
forgotten . . .
           I am trying to understand
what happened, rather, what *didn't* happen next.
Our slap was inertia, discourtesy, silence.
Impassive and frivolous, we froze her out
with mineral indolence deeper than self-love
—that gladly would have seen the stars go snuff before
it chose to move one inch. The stars that night shone true.

—And glimmer high above her cohort of the hunt.
(So it is I imagined the harsh event.)
Black branches at midnight in the hostile grove,
stones some women grope along, and famished wind
tears flame from the meager fires and out-howls
their cries; they huddle and with warm bodies shield
the white-daubed effigy of the goddess their queen.
Poor and frightened, unprotected, prey themselves,
how it crazes them to have to keep alive
in their own weak words—like a seed of outrage,
a violent growth—the abandoned consciences
and lost concern of unprincipled and selfish men!
And now she comes in, gasping her story, she feels
she must, she must give birth to a chunk of metal,
this humiliation she bears and never,
not so long as she lives, forgets.

3

                    She stood.
It was not what one had expected, that look
around the room that said she could as well
go hunt in a barn as do her hunting here,
potshots that we were, pitiful sport,
and really couldn't give a damn about
us dodos either way—redeemed in spades
or sent to bull among the shades—we were just
in the way of the chaste and fierce pursuit,

shutting her view to the clear way and great use,
and deflecting with our huge, torpid auras
the shining crowd of spiritual arrows
sweeping through the high trees.
                              Naked, bright, serene,
something moved there (I saw), someone swift—tempest
of moonlight—pattered over the leaves and lit
the lost traces to delight where they were touched.
Darkness came rushing after.
                              I rejoined our pack
—Sidney and Charles, Melvin, Arthur, Andrew—
to hound and lacerate with muttered slurs
the high arch and light heel of her tall,
unsullied shadow where she descended
the creaking stair—as if we wished to merit
in full measure the judgment against us
and with negligent, grinning jeers dishonored hope
for that rebirth we could not cease to crave or fear.

4

Or was it only an evening
of moral melodrama we craved?
I'm not that certain what went on.
I got carried away—let's say—
but not so far that I don't wake up
mornings to Diana's mantle lost
in sun, and dailiness everywhere,
our comedy-as-usual,
the world just chugging off
down the laff-track of the days,
rollicking on regular—you know
the blend: optimism and bad faith,
or something too muddled to be quite that.
Sometimes I see her in the corridors,
taping a placard to the wall
or loping along, her old fatigues
resurrected as white overalls.
Let's see, it's a feminist event

the posters cheerily advertise.
Or announce her poets' workshop
for women only, Wednesday evenings
in some *not* suburban living room.
I think she likes the business
—her greetings (across a distance
neither infringes) now feature
a neat, cryptic nod. *Cosa nostra.*
She could add a smile, it wouldn't hurt.
Her new poems seem not all that bad,
though hardly less conventional for all
their energy. Why tell her that?
Her thesis—so Ginny says—progresses.
"Venus and Nietzsche in Paris."
Maybe I didn't understand a thing.
And Melvin, Sidney, Charles, Arthur
(Andrew now bulls among the shades
—in Berkeley, where else?),
when I ask them what they recall
of that evening and do they think
it was wild or what, every man jack
answers, "Huh?" while an innocent blank
endearingly dulls his everyday face.
Is one to infer that after all
other versions are being versed?
Almost anything seems to go
—if you don't lose faith in yourself.
You can screw your neighbor, okay,
but keep the old conscience clean.
I suppose you think that's sad.

Of course, I see the moon, too,
every now and then, still shining so
I have to lift up face and voice
and blare to her with open throat
the full song of my heart's adoring
—as any one of us might want to do.

Summer's Sublet

(hath all too short a date)

He felt he was carrying her whole place
uphill on his back, bearing it in mind
. . . the badly gored leather of the easy chair,
the scratches flocking along the table top,
or the fridge's all but terminal *râle*,
the slim venetian's elegant droopy slat
—these fragilities of a large "efficiency"
which he was shepherding for an old friend,
taking them to feed in the high summer pastures,
preserving them for one more season still
from time's furtive, undelicate claws,
or his own never ill-intentioned carelessness.

Still he was bumping into things.
As if blindness had redecorated the room,
nothing there seemed meant to put itself on view,
the watery, green mirror was so shy a thing
he kept on losing it in the cloud-white wall
because nowhere could he find himself—and yet
he stuck out painfully, that much he *felt*.
How one is *de trop* in another's life!
—not the blank mermaid of fairy tales, of course,
waiting to have her features drawn in fresh ink,
but a face already complete with erosions,
such vaguenesses, regrets, apologies . . .
Oh, on the contrary—he found himself
wanting to say, hand splayed over his heart—
on the contrary, it is I who am too solid.
Imagine, talking to furniture like that!

*   *   *

The furniture found a way to talk back.
The phone spent all one night calling him up,
and then pretended not to know his name.
Surely it was alive, he could hear it breathing.
The fridge, too, played dead, though its body was warm.
He wasn't fooled, not for a second—but
how a small thing can turn you upside down!

Another night someone hammered suddenly
on the door, shouted *Help*, ran down the hall
to the next door, pounded again . . .
In this metropolis the cry of distress
terrified more than the terror it fled . . .
One more midnight dropped blackly over him
like a hanged man's hood: the loneliness was
absolute—but soiled, used, full of last breaths.

Things were in that room he could hardly approach,
and places shuddering with life of their own.
He felt an infant Jonah battered by
the peristalsis of her spirit's labors,
by soundings cold and sharp against his ears . . .
Here she'd sat doing the sums of her life.
Or lay on the narrow cot under the stormy
air conditioner, praying for her daughter
that she might be happy, and less brusque with her.
At this small, white table, eating alone,
she reviewed the ranks of her obligations
and found them present and in proper order,
then forgave this injury, renewed that pardon.
Her magnanimity once more surprised her.
For one happy moment everything was clear
and able to look after itself—she was free,
truly free, as maybe not since she was a child.
Between coffee and a last scotch-and-water,
she canceled as entirely inconsequential
a longstanding debt of her own.

Halfway to the sink on the worn parquet,
a sudden thought rattled the cup she carried
and she sat quickly to catch her breath.
"A life, a life, a *whole life*," she gasped, "*my* life!"
Where did that happen? In that chair? Or in this?
He jumped up, walked, stood, couldn't sit still . . .
Like a pet turned suddenly savage, one favored,
old regret bit her deeply while she stared,
over the faucet's roar, into the corner of
an empty shelf . . .
                            And late one night
he saw the white invisible gardenia
on the inside of the refrigerator door,
the photo lost from the dresser drawer
she mourned like the child itself . . .

Every day now he found something else missing:
books gone from the year before, he was sure of it,
paintings bartered for emptiness . . . and what remained
had that remnant look—of being no one's,
or nothing, dispossessed of identity,
like orphans, at once touched by the gods—sacred—
and dispirited . . .
                            But why was she doing it?
Was it restless old age in her, impatient
to harry and rend clear through its withered root?
a kind of mad rushing around—so little held
one down—in a rage to tear loose completely
and be swept away . . . ?
Or her abandonment of the day on the day
she understood it could take place without her?
that her consciousness no longer was required
by the world for the world to be the world?
He pictured her off in her northern summer now,
unencumbered and concentrating all her thought
to lower the doorsill, to ease the step down.

*   *   *

How calm she seemed just then, and high—shining out
to him, like a pale flare drifting luminous
over the vacant sea long after . . .

"But *why?* Why *me?*" He looked around the room again.
"And whose little boy are *you?*" he asked the one
in the mirror, bereft, startled, one hand half raised.
It was too much—more than he could take—to be
the recipient of her eternal goodbye
aimed vaguely toward the place where he happened to be,
too much to have to stand there and wave back slowly,
relinquished though he was with the rest, and all
his human powers reduced to helplessness
by life that didn't want to be saved . . .

He gave up his sublet suddenly, and fled.

The Call

On the phone from Florida, it's Louie,
nearly a cousin, almost long-lost.
There's something important he wants to know,
after all these years. I hear it in his voice.
It's like he's put a package down and looks up
and he sees sky, horizon, trees, something
empty, endless, peaceful, always the same.
"It hit me all of a sudden.
Listen, Charlie, don't worry about me.
I don't second guess myself anymore.
I'm sure I made the right decisions.
Really, people can envy me,
I've been as lucky as hell:
I got my health and all,
I'm like a bull I'm so strong,
I could live forever if I had to,
Charlie—honest I could."
But underneath, there's something else.
Shy, puzzled, urgent is how he sounds. I find
I'm bending over the phone to get closer.
"So how are things? What's going on?"
and then so low I've got to hold my breath
to hear, "Charlie, tell me," he whispers,
"how . . . how's the weather up there?"
I guess he's asking about the family
he left behind—do they miss him,
the wind and the rain and snow,
the immortals from long ago? and after all
what good would it be to survive alone?
And so I tell him what he wants to hear,
"Lousy, Lou, the weather's worse every year."

III THE FLIGHT FROM THE CITY

The Flight from the City

Each man on the street insists he is himself,
but all have in common the same double: Disaster.

"*Very good.*
Now, once more.
Your name, please."

"Kleinwort.
I mean, Hummingblood.
Yes, Hummingblood!—I *think.*
Because I, too, was asking,
'Who am I? Myself? Or my double?
Hummingblood in fact or "Hummingblood" in quotes?
The real one or the substitute?
—who shadows me at a distance sometimes,
or stalks me from inside my clothes,
jostling to take over my flannel trousers,
my blazer, my boxer shorts, my spats.
Well, I may be either one, or both, in fact,
a shadow in shoes and socks, so to speak.
This book will know . . .'—this very book you see.
Names have been in here since time began."

Since time began . . . had I seen anyone like this?
—Orange hairpiece like a haggard cockatoo's,
some dribbled calligraphies of greasy fard
that glossed his eyes' effect of fevered death,
the Doric sideburns daubed in sickening shoe wax
lifting heavenward his temples and his brow.
And this was the pitiful material
my "workshop" had to make do with
—some mannikin on whom the heavens had fallen,
who was himself a splinter of crashing sky,
a giggle rippling the face of the void.

But I was patient. I went on.
"Splendid.
Very *good.*
Now, what happened next?"

"I was a wobbling rim around
a cinema's bright spokes and went
wheeling up the smoky night. Then down from
the zenith, weightless, blind, my body unreeled:
the screen over which empty spasms of light
and darkness staggered through unending war.
My way was that occluded, obscure—as if
I dreamed it all inside another's sleep . . .
till nightmare—mine or someone's—of consciousness
without remission woke me to a world without
dimension, or limit . . . out of nowhere
images came crashing into my eyes
under the clicking cold sidereal grid . . .
Traffic lights patrolled the heedless dark . . .

"On the street I saw these things, these things.
Live graffiti rotted on the walls, writhed,
throbbed in dark peristalses, then slithered,
convulsive arabesques that shivered in place,
went nowhere, waved their flagella, wove
their ornaments, invited one in to the heart
of their rouge insignia, the bold misspellings
—all lip, cilia, tentacles, tongue summoning you
to be the substance in their self-caresses . . .
Rats and jackals sat looking up,
slavering for them to drop . . .
I had awakened—not to shut my eyes again—
to disaster. And fire everywhere."

"And where *was this? Where were* you?"

"Marauding beacons overhead ravaged the dark sky
or smashed themselves on cloud into high headlines

about the famous strangers we would never meet,
their names the common prayer in our divided night.
And sudden—now incessant—criss-
crossing clamor: sirens claxons wailing bells.
The acoustic graffiti of a savage officialdom
were tearing clear across the shuddering rubble,
a vast sheol in which the City lay foundered.
Was it already blasted and trashed?
and surviving as the audience spellbound
before the footage of its legendary demise,
wailing and applauding as they died?
As for me that night, although I was there,
nothing there seemed my own experience
but just more news, things neither true nor false
but life at a long distance arriving as
the morning headline folded beside the coffee cup.

"And then the street assaulted me.
The mugger messages came for my soul,
pressing their hot slogans to my throat,
whispering, '*Give* it to us, *give* it to us!'
I turned my pockets out. 'Empty! Empty!'
my pockets cried, 'See, I have no soul.'
I disclaimed ever having known me.
Sundering myself, I surrendered him and sped on,
deaf to the scuffle and screams behind.
Who me, a victim? Never! I'm the *other* guy!
No, I proclaimed my predator's grin and whistle,
my hard logo of self-advèrtisement
—violent of color, virulent in stink.
I became inedible like an auto.
I posed as an identity posing as
a value—but what was I worth to anyone?"

And what was the meaning of his sudden smile?
Slugging assassins with pillows, was he?
Putting down murderers with mental weathers?

My associate and I exchanged a glance
—Have we gotten our hands on the wrong party?

"A thrill of silliness went lilting,
then sank itself to the hilt in me.
I was hysteria in slow motion,
transition in transit,
a shattered mirror shambling down the street,
setting one image before the other,
consuming and relinquishing sight after sight.
Constant voiding and betrayal of the past.
Panic of consumption, flight through things.
It was so hard to be serious,
to see how any life could matter.
If the world had decided to do itself in,
it wasn't up to me to tell it no.
I could go along with that.
I mean, Was I *supposed* to mind?
But if this really was the end of everything,
somebody out there ought to know it,
and surely it was worthy of transmission,
the roar and outcries and lamentation thrilling
outward on empty airwaves beyond the stars.
Maybe the media that catered reality
were beginning to cater the apocalypse.
Hadn't they pointed sparking wands and all at once
it occurred to thousands, yes, really, they
were feeling tired and would—as if it were
the most natural thing in the world—lie down
on the street in broad daylight and, well, nap a bit?
Such a good idea: to just drop dead right there!
And what harm if one should steal away too soon
one's little winks from all eternity?
It was montage anyway, lamination
of shadow and flame—the difference between life
and death was immaterial, just no big deal,
a budget item in someone's big bucks fantasy.
Then the street blurred, and ran like ink.

*   *   *

"There was no sensation of touching ground.
Adrift in a soup of lingos, sloshing
severed tongues sliding all together
or soddenly ironizing in my cheek.
Things I meant I didn't mean I meant.
The words I kept taking back were not my words.
Had I been expropriated? No self now?
no prohibited sanctum? merely a set
of always negotiable positions
of diminishing liability?
To be at last immortal and a nought?
And in my skull's bare ruined cinema,
now what low insistent hissing hushing?
whose sweet sinister hot licks?
　　Sucks.
　　Say what?
　　That stuff sucks.
　　Huh?
　　Get with it, Chuck!
　　You ain't you
　　—you just your jive.
　　Same as I.
　　That's why we gots to deal it, daddy.
　　You hear me talk?
　　I mean, you hustle it, baby,
　　put its ass to work!
　　You dig me, Buck?
　　Hey, Humanbutt gots to die,
　　but *you* some other guy—dig?
　　'Cause, shhiiit, son,
　　when that mother don't cut it,
　　you dump him, pops, you split,
　　I mean, scrap your rap, pappy,
　　blow yourself a different riff,
　　get you some *new* sweet nut.
　　I said, Now move it!
　　You *dig?*

Get your shit together, Sid!
Get with it, Chuck!

"Oh yes, Hummingblood was up for grabs."

"And you, it appears, had loosened your grip.
Or were you perhaps someone else
—if you were anyone at all?"

"Yes, of course, there might be two—or
there might be two thousand—of me,
but only one Hummingblood *by right*,
and all the others a nonce vernacular
dying on the air, poor wanderers
shaken nameless from the exploded town
who would be Hummingblood to be anyone.
And all are lost if one is lost,
and no one saved unless all are saved.
That night the elements were running for their lives
—while I thrashed, jerked, shook, fell inside my clothes,
struggling to bind again the missing pages of
our *Book of Every Name of All the People,*
where, leaf by leaf, life by life, we were
awaited and greeted, and our names and place
reserved and lavished to us before our births.

"But somewhere I, too, was being quoted,
somewhere they were saying, 'Hummingblood,'
somewhere commas were being inverted about me,
excerpting me from the context of my name
and rendering me a sign to be interpreted
to myself, whatever any noisy expert,
all the suave managers of meaning,
would say I was."

He twisted his neck as if
he meant to look around: half of one wide eye
rotated my way, half his mouth spat words at me.

*   *   *

"But your henchman here, this Hurtingbrute,
who wrenches arms from sockets, breaks heads apart,
this Hurtingbrute scrapes his horrid pate caustic white,
sculpting from a human brow the skull's abstraction
—being sergeant of its dismal ultimate cult,
into whose long ranks he crams his limp recruits.
He calls it sacrifice, calls it *self*-sacrifice
to boot: having renounced the right to exist,
Hurtingbrute acquires the right to be lethal.

"So this much I knew:
I had to recollect the book in which
we are and I am—and then, wherever
my eyes would take me, flee with it!"

He sagged abruptly—in lieu of toppling over—
but drew himself up before assistance reached him,
with courage not unequal to his suffering.
Nor could I withhold my admiration
—a feeling almost too fraternal.

"Then graffiti again.
Gorging on the verbal detritus.
Would nothing else survive?
All night long empty trains rushed
in narrow corridors underground.
Of course, the furious graffiti
had set them going, drove them on
—thunderous fugues of script,
a last vandal hand's grimy shriek
to the far termini of the City.
At eye level, in dawn's new pearl, I saw
across the towers' flickering imagery
a sludge and flotsam of names was stretched
—as if the tideline of a tarry surf
had left a heraldry in living carcasses,
a reef

of rabid telephones and raucous codpieces,
coral carapaces of logos,
and lurid solipsistic flora,
and raw genitalia dripping initials:
unanswered messages vexed to reiteration,
to self-elaboration, to self-quotation.
Jungle of identities without being.
(I stopped my ears and broadcast a din inwardly
—my head bloated with noise that might be me.
I'm no fool, I wore my coat of graffiti
and strode about like a public urinal.)

"A nobility of the poor had flourished there.
Warrior-poets clutched their juvenile scrota
and screamed their primping names at nothingness.
From the foot-square kingdom of a scrawl,
they bawled their barbarian's nostalgia for
the lost heroic eras of property
(the poor are always with us, always out of date).
Their baffled scribbles were demanding answers:
Who signs and authorizes reality here?
Isn't anybody *boss* in this City?
Why only *managers* everywhere?
Who *owns* this place?
What blind bitched-up fucked-over god built here?
—the unfeatured blocks where nothing loves the eye,
this big dead stone page, its desolated names
of reality, and smooth facades praying, Gouge,
give me life!
            —This was the unresisting blank
they desecrated: they staked their claim, they dared
the absentee god in his bland disguises.
Sly or shy, the god would not come out
or show any face but their own defacings."

He seemed more thoughtful now, better spoken,
less nervous, silly, inconsequent
—or, rather, less undemandingly obscure,

as if it might matter to him that his words
might matter to others, for all that his fingers
continued drifting through invisible pages.

"The gods had absconded from our city
and carried off with them the good words
enchanting the altars and effigies.
Animals through whom we joined the whole
of creation had run away from us to hide.
The elements all were lost in darkness.
And ourselves in our multitude, the crowd
of us pulsating and alive with our
individual visions of the crowd of us
—was now its negative crowd panicking in place,
among whom I turned aimlessly in the plaza.
What then might elevate our miserable cries?

"I, too, felt the city's acquiescence,
and rapture, in ruin. I, too, wished
the end to come quickly; our concern
and constancy—our being human—
had been too little to hold us together;
so many abandoned, so much forgotten.
Then let the city be one again in destruction!
I prayed for the unbinding of the elements,
the wind unable to overtake the wind,
the wave wandering lonely in the street.
And went out with the others to welcome disaster,
obliteration of our disheartened sentences,
the devastation of our indifference
—let this debris of feeling be offered to flame!
I stood with the jubilant ruined survivors
exhibiting our wounds—See, here fire
touched, here earth's heavy hand came down—
while we gasped, I have . . . lost . . . *everything.*
I, too, in the crowd escaping toward ruin . . .

"But who was this choir I howled among?"

*   *   *

"I hope, Hummingblood—or Kleinwort,—you don't mean
to embarrass our proceeding with confessions.
If so, you have misunderstood, I regret
to say, the purpose of your interrogation
—as you seem still to comprehend imperfectly
that your search to recover your originals
is itself quite sadly unoriginal,
a shadow of the initial fall and fissure.
—'Accept no substitutes'? That is the motto of
a world where there are only substitutes.
Now, think where you are, to whom you speak.
Reply accordingly. Consider that
it may not be your answers we require."

"A little word pecks among the blowing pages
of the scattered nomenclature . . .
Just Kleinwort, doubled over, trying
to put this and this and this together.
An insect circles on the facade of ruin.
It was somebody or other on his belly
in the slime and mother of origins
—it was me
where I lay and listened for the first story:
New Life Out of Old Death,
a spring in the dark stubble,
the birth bubbling up.
Stubble? Shadows were leaping
from the tall flame-towers, dust
sang in the mouths of the choruses,
burst, the matrix spilled brine out,
the clans and quarters were shattered.
A world was in ruins.
But nothing moved and grew in death.
Neither was death itself there.
—Ruin had become the system.
Irresistible to itself,
the manic short-circuit was wheeling

through perpetual motion pictures where
a world of fungibles whirled in a dead flame
—shadow and darkness, substitute, shade . . .
Terror was to know nothing outside.
In terror, I knew I was a mannikin
on whom the heavens had fallen
and was myself a splinter of crashing sky,
a giggle rippling the face of the void.
In terror, then, I understood
I was the system thinking Hummingblood.
Terrified, I felt it spoil my lungs,
the final excrement of stone-filled air,
clotted omens I would be compelled to become . . .

"Was resistance my way out
—refuse the labyrinth,
be unthinkable, become
silence, cipher, grit, be
the word lost from every language?
Be namelessness?
Then no one would be Hummingblood.
I hid among my shadows.
I was scared.
I wished I would die right there.
There they found me.
I was hurled in spirals
winding in to a navel, a narrow pit.
Nose to wall, spread-eagle
against the clay, naked—here
they manacle me, pinion, mock, flay
with questions."

      *"Welcome—once more! We have
so few visitors. Few come this far."*

            "And who
are you to whom I owe my salvation?"

*   *   *

"And why not your salvation?
Aren't these rags I wear the rags you wore?
Aren't the pages of your book
this tremendous autumn on the floor?
Isn't mine the name you were looking for?
Don't you recognize me?
*Inspector Harmingbad—*à votre service—
formerly your baby brother, now
of the City's constabulary.
You are, as you understand, in the City.
You never left it.
The City dreamed you ... child,
arrayed you in a dreamlike flame,
foretold your long way stumbling here, and told
you over and over. You were its story,
The Lost Redeeming Enemy: suppressed revised
corrupted purged rewritten forgotten revived
mutilated robbed botched burned scattered interred
forged falsified denied—and in every version
true, and each time more true, its only truth
and one hope. Therefore the hope it sacrifices.
Now the City salutes and embraces you
with its most ironic citation: Spikes Paired.
So, say you are pleased to see me!"

"Better pleased now than yesterday,
since sight has scratched away my eyes.
I have hid my silence in volubility.
Now I brandish it for all to hear."

"Indeed. I hear you perfectly.
Of course, I wished—I wish—to know nothing.
This inquiry has undertaken, rather,
to establish the integrity of your
resistance, which I require—I demand it—that I
may capture myself at the wall of your will
and know I haven't vanished in my system.
My 'paranoia'? Spare me the vulgar drivel.

I hunt down and persecute my enemies
in order to resurrect more *murderous mobs*
of howling martyrs beyond the system.
I press their execrations to my throat,
am justified by their just indignation
—these are sweet air and green ground to me, I
the living pinnacle on the heap of your dead.
Here, now, I rise in the dark margin
—this danger—and I shine between
the everlasting day of the system's
entire annihilating illumination and
the flicker of my enemy's moonstruck knife.

"Like you I am famished,
like you I rage, for reality.
Terror is to rage unopposed.
Poor whoever-you-are
(your double's double's double, after all)
who this last evening of earth
have learned in your little flesh
how—deep within the City, beneath
the system's ghostly totality—
driven by the voltage of domination,
the old technology ticks on:
one man is beating another.
What do you feel? What are you?
—when my demiurge strikes.
This fascinates as if it might hold at once
the secret of freedom, the secret of fate,
something unnegotiable and mortal in me.
To feel what you feel at the point
where flesh fails and mind faints
and my will is nothing but my will:
so I submit to my power
so I resist it.
When the gods vanish, pain becomes the god,
the indwelling alien,
the purest resistance

to the shortest circuit,
term to every terminology.

"And you imagined no substitute
would follow you this far, little one?
or follow and not *go farther?*
Yes, I am running on ahead now . . .

"Now give *it to me, your silence . . . brother!*
Say nothing more—whatever may occur.
Be my witness I neither flinch nor squeal.
Quickly: nod if you don't *understand.*
Good.
     Come, Hurtingbrute, your tongs . . ."

BUT HUMMINGBLOOD SCREAMED FOR THE SAKE OF HARMINGBAD'S
    SOUL.

IV

Art of the Haiku

His finger then, now yours
here, where master stopped, went back,
counted syllables.

2 - 2/08